The Odd Job Man
and the
Thousand Mile
Boots

Story by Jean Kenward
Pictures by Val Biro

Oxford University Press

Once, there was an Odd Job Man who had lived for many years in the same village. There was always plenty to do. One day, he might be mending a smashed window, another replacing a broken tile or repairing a gate latch. He never knew what would come next.

One morning, as he was sharpening a lawn mower, a
swallow spoke to him. 'You are always in the same
place,' twittered the swallow. 'Don't you ever want to
see the world like I do?'

The Odd Job Man thought for a bit. 'I might travel one day,' he muttered to himself. 'But only if I could get to the end of the world and back by sunset. For I do like my own bed.'

He made up his mind to rise early next Tuesday, and borrow a pair of thousand—mile—boots from the giant who lived in the churchyard.

 The giant was kind and friendly, though it was a nuisance that he bit pieces out of the tombstones now and then. He had to be reminded not to do it. He slept in the church itself, with his head stuck up into the steeple. There was nowhere else large enough for him to lie down in, except the police station; and that had no spire.

 When the Odd Job Man turned up soon after sunrise on Tuesday the giant was asleep and snoring so loudly that the windows rattled, and the organ too. His feet were sticking out of the doorway. He had taken his boots off, and, I am sorry to say, his socks had holes in them, as big as turnips.

 Somehow or other, he had to be woken. But no amount of pushing and pinching made any difference.

 The giant slept on . . .

'I shall have to leave a note,' the Odd Job Man decided at last. There was a stub of pencil in his pocket, and a paper bag with liquorice allsorts in it. He tipped the sweets out, and wrote on the paper.

Have borrowed boots. Please. Thank you. Back at sunset.

Then he arranged the sweets in a pattern on top of the note to stop it blowing away, and pulled on the boots.

Of course they fitted perfectly. For they were magic, and would have fitted anybody.

On and on he strode, a
thousand miles at a step,
through grapes and
pineapples, icicles and
penguins. He passed over the
Sahara desert at five to ten,
and the peaks of Everest at
five past. He saw eagles and
elephants, ostriches and I
don't know what. It is a long
way to the end of the world.

By midday he was weary, and having drunk a
whole bottle of lemonade at a swig, he settled
himself comfortably beside a river, took off his
boots, dangled his feet in the water, and dozed
off . . .

. . . When he opened his eyes, the boots had gone.
  He looked absolutely everywhere, and trudged
quite a long distance in his socks, searching. His feet
became hot and sore.

'I know where the boots are,' shrilled
a spider. 'But I'm too busy to say. I
must get on with my web. I have to
finish by nightfall, and have no time
for gossip.'

'I know where they are,' grunted
a leopard, sneaking through the trees.
'But I can't stop now – I'm hunting.
Keep out of my way!'

'I know where they are!' squawked a high-up voice. It was a parrot. 'I saw. I see everything. Crocodile took them. He went down the river, in that direction.' He pointed with his wing.

'Thank you!' cried the Odd Job Man, joyfully. 'I will offer him my last sandwich, if only he will give them back.'

The Odd Job Man trudged on. By now, he was limping a little; but soon he came to a group of monkeys, eating nuts and throwing down the shells.

'A crocodile with boots?' they jabbered. 'We saw him. He went this way . . . he went that way . . . he dropped one. We tried it on. It fits us all – the left foot, that is to say. But we don't want it. We will gladly exchange it for your haversack. It would be ideal for storing nuts.'

The Odd Job Man took the last sandwich out of his bag, and the last bottle of lemonade. He stuffed them in his pockets. The monkeys ran to snatch the haversack, and threw down the boot.

'He's gone that way,' they chattered, pointing.

And the Odd Job Man limped on.

At last – at long last – he saw the boot sticking out of the water, and the jaws of a crocodile round it! The crocodile was trying to swallow it, but as it was a magic boot, it wouldn't go down. It seemed to get stuck on his back teeth. His wife was terribly cross.

'It's your own fault. I told you so,' she grunted. 'But you wouldn't listen. You should have eaten the Odd Job Man instead. He looked tasty. As it happens, I can see him clumping up by the river right now.'

When the Odd Job Man heard this he was so
dreadfully frightened that his teeth chattered.
He hiccuped once, twice, three times, and had
to take a long swallow of lemonade to calm
himself. Luckily, hiccups are catching. Did you
know that? Mr Crocodile was really hungry as
well as thirsty by now. And he hiccuped too! It
was a bit like an earthquake.

And out fell the magic boot!

Luckily it floated. It was very, very near to Mr and Mrs
Crocodile, but the Odd Job Man was feeling a little
braver – well, just a little. He held his last sandwich far
out over the water with one hand . . . and gently,
dropped it . . .

'Delicious!' snorted Mr Crocodile. And he swam peacefully off, munching. With a swish of her tail his wife went down to the bottom of the river to search for crumbs.

Whew! It had been a narrow escape.

The Odd Job Man ran and ran, from today into
yesterday and back again. It was hot, then
cold . . . then warm . . . then windy . . . and
there in the churchyard was the amiable giant
mending his socks with some hairy rope
threaded through a skewer. He had cut his toe
nails too, and piled them up neatly beside him in
a heap, until the dustbin people should come.
They looked like bicycle mudguards.

    He was especially pleased to pull on his boots
again, for he fancied a little stroll before bedtime:
perhaps to Australia and back.

'What was it like?' he boomed, in his huge, huge voice. 'Your day off?'

'The same as most days,' answered the Odd Job Man. 'But more exciting. The same, you might say, only different. You see, we don't keep crocodiles here.'

He put on his own boots – lace-ups they were, I believe – and stuck his hands into his pockets.

'Goodnight,' he called. 'See you!' . . . and whistled his way home.